Hostage

by

Malorie Blackman

Illustrated by Derek Brazell

For Neil and Elizabeth, with love

Published in Great Britain by Barrington Stoke Ltd
10 Belford Terrace, Edinburgh, EH4 3DQ
First published in *Amazing Adventure Stories*
edited by Tony Bradman (Transworld, 1994)
Copyright © 1999 Oneta Malorie Blackman
Illustrations © Derek Brazell
The moral right of the author has been asserted in
accordance with the Copyright, Designs and
Patents Act 1988
ISBN 1-902260-12-0

Printed by Polestar AUP Aberdeen Limited
Printed 1999 (four times)
The publisher acknowledges subsidy from the Scottish Arts Council
towards the publication of this volume

THE SCOTTISH ARTS COUNCIL

Meet The Author - Malorie Blackman

What is your favourite animal?
Alsatian dog
What is your favourite boy's name?
Dominic
What is your favourite girl's name?
Elizabeth
What is your favourite food?
Ben and Jerry's Cherry
Garcia Ice-cream
What is your favourite music?
'Love will find a way'
by Lionel Richie
What is your favourite hobby?
Playing computer games

Meet The Illustrator - Derek Brazell

What is your favourite animal?
Cairn Terrier
What is your favourite boy's name?
Raul
What is your favourite girl's name?
Siân
What is your favourite food?
Chocolate
What is your favourite music?
Pop music
What is your favourite hobby?
Listening to music and
visiting friends

Barrington Stoke was a famous and much loved story-teller. He travelled from village to village, carrying a lantern to light his way. He arrived as it grew dark and when the young boys and girls of the village saw the glow of his lantern, they hurried to the central meeting place. They were full of excitement and expectation, for his stories were always wonderful.

Then Barrington Stoke set down his lantern. In the flickering light the listeners were enthralled by his tales of adventure, horror and mystery. He knew exactly what they liked best and he loved telling a good story. And another. And then another. When the lantern burned low and dawn was nearly breaking, he slipped away. He was gone by morning, only to appear the next day in some other village to tell the next story.

Contents

Chapter 1
Kidnap

When I left school, it was nearly dark. I zipped my anorak right up to my chin and I wondered what to do next. I wasn't going back to our house, that was for sure. As I kicked through the snow, I decided to go to Deansea High Street for an ice-cream and then maybe the cinema. That way I could put off seeing Dad. I didn't want to see him at all – not after the blazing row we'd had that morning before I left for school.

1

I hated our house, I never called it home. Now that Mum had gone, it was always so lonely, so desperately quiet. Even when Dad and I were together, we never seemed to have much to say to each other.

I dug into my pockets and found two safety pins, a cracked mirror, chewing gum, my comb, the end of a pencil, my house keys – but not much money. So much for going to the cinema! Just an ice-cream then!

"Angela? Angela Henshaw?"

At the sound of my name, I turned. A woman with short, brown hair smiled at me from behind the wheel of a blue Rover. I'd never seen her before, so how did she know my name? I stopped walking. She stopped the car, although the engine was still running.

"Angela Henshaw?" she said again.

"Yeah?" I replied hesitantly.

From out of nowhere, a warm, rough hand that smelt of petrol was clamped over my mouth and an arm braced around my waist like a vice. Before I could even blink, I was lifted off my feet. I could hear a man's voice behind me, but I couldn't make out what he was saying over the sound of my heart slamming against my ribs. By the time I thought to struggle and kick, I'd been bundled into the car and, with a screech of brakes, it went tearing down the road.

Chapter 2
Blind Panic

It all happened so quickly.

I looked around, my head jerking like a puppet's. A blond man in a light grey raincoat sat on my right, a bald man in a navy blue leather jacket sat on my left. I was jammed between them so tightly, I felt like toothpaste being squeezed out of a tube.

Terrified, I opened my mouth and *screamed*. Just as loud as I could. But I only got out about three seconds' worth before the bald guy clamped his hand over my mouth.

"SHUT UP!" he hissed at me.

His breath smelt of garlic, his fingers of petrol. I tried to scream through his fingers but the air rushed back into my throat, making me cough.

"Listen to me," said Baldy. "We're not going to hurt you. We just want to make sure your Dad does as he's told. As soon as he does, we'll let you go. Understand?"

I didn't answer. I *couldn't.* The way my stomach was turning over, if I opened my mouth I'd be sick.

"Don't scream again, or else ..." said the other man, the blond, with icy blue eyes. Baldy slowly began to remove his fingers from over my mouth. I opened my mouth to scream again.

I didn't even get one second's worth out this time. Baldy's fingers were back over my mouth.

"Right. If that's the way you want it," he said, glaring at me.

His hand over my mouth was pressing down so hard, it hurt. His thick fingers covered my nostrils as well as my mouth. I couldn't breathe. My lungs were going to burst. I tried pulling at his fingers with both of my hands but he just clamped down harder. I looked up at him, my eyes stinging with tears. He frowned at me, then relaxed his grip slightly. I tilted my head back, dragging air down into my lungs. I wanted to scream and shout and throw myself at the car doors.

I kept telling myself, don't panic ... keep calm ... think ... The words filled my head as I tried, without success, to stop myself from shaking like a leaf. What should I do?

"That's better, Angela," said Baldy softly. "Just do as we say and we'll all be better off."

"In more ways than one!" laughed the blond man. His smug, vicious laugh sent an icy chill down my spine.

I looked out of the windows, ready to throw myself at one of the car doors to attract

someone's attention the moment I had the
chance, but the driver knew Deansea very well.
She kept to the back streets where there were
very few people and no traffic lights around.

What should I do?

Baldy had spoken of Dad doing something they wanted. Was that why they'd grabbed me? It had to be. Dad was the owner of the best jewellery shop in Deansea. I'd always reckoned that Dad chose the jewellery business when he left the army, because that way he wouldn't be bothered with children. Dad didn't like children.

The car jolted, bringing me back to the present and my awful situation. *Do something!*

We finally left Deansea by the old church road.

"Blindfold her," the woman commanded.

The blond man pulled out a dirty grey scarf from behind him.

"Do we really have to do that?" frowned Baldy. "We'll be gone long before they find her. What does it matter if she sees where we're going?"

The woman glared at him. "Do as I say," she ordered, before turning back to the road.

"No! NO!" I screamed.

I couldn't help it. I freaked. No way was I going to let them blindfold me without a fight. I kicked and hit out as hard as I could. Baldy grabbed me by the arms, his grip like a vice. The blond man tried to get the blindfold over my eyes anyway, so the moment one of his hands came within range I bit down – *hard*. He swore, then grabbed me away from Baldy and shook me until my teeth rattled.

"Do that again and I'll make sure your Dad never sees you again. Not in one piece. D'you understand?" he hissed.

I didn't answer.

"UNDERSTAND?" he shouted.

I nodded, terrified.

"Good. Now keep still," he said.

I couldn't have moved then, even if my life depended on it. I remembered how only a while ago, I'd not wanted to go home because I didn't want to see Dad. Now I wondered if I'd ever see him again.

Chapter 3
Countdown

They were after Dad's jewels – they had to be. But there was one big question. Would Dad really hand over all his precious jewels just for me? After our blazing row that morning, I really wasn't sure that he would. And it wasn't just this morning. It seemed like ever since Mum left, Dad and I had done nothing *but* quarrel.

You're not beaten yet, I thought desperately. Don't panic and stay alert.

But it was so hard. My heart was still bouncing about in my chest and my stomach was turning over like a tumble dryer.

The first thing to do was to work out where I was. I tried to think clearly. I tilted my head up slightly but I couldn't see under the blindfold. Now what?

Well ... we'd taken the old church road and since they'd blindfolded me, we'd been travelling for at least three minutes. How fast? Not as fast as Dad when he drove, so less than forty miles an hour? I couldn't be sure.

I started to count. When I'd reached six hundred, the car turned left. I started counting from one again, slow and steady, counting off the seconds. It was a trick Dad had been taught in the army. The only time we didn't seem to argue was when he was telling stories about his time in the army.

More counting. The road seemed to wind a bit but the car didn't slow down to make a proper turn until I reached one thousand four hundred, then it turned right. I counted to one hundred and twenty before the car turned right again. We must have turned onto a track or a field because the car, and everyone in it, bounced up and down as if we were all on a trampoline.

And all the time, no one in the car said a word. I tried to memorise the route we were taking, like memorising the numbers to open a safe. Six hundred left, fourteen hundred right, one hundred and twenty right.

Suddenly the car stopped and the engine was turned off. I looked around as if to see through the scarf covering my eyes. The car doors opened. I sat still, listening to my kidnappers get out of the car.

"This way."

Someone grabbed my left arm and pulled me out of the car. The snow was fresher here than in town. It crunched under my wellies. I heard the wind whistling in some tall trees to my right. We turned left and started walking. After ten steps the ground became firm as we entered some kind of building. I heard a door shut behind me. I'd never been so frightened by the sound of a door closing before.

After five steps, Baldy said gruffly, "Stairs!"

I lifted my feet higher and started climbing up some steps. Twelve in all, the fifth one creaked.

At the top of the stairs I was led into another room. I stood still.

"C-Can I t-take my blindfold off n-now?" I whispered, my hands moving up towards my eyes.

No one stopped me so I pulled off the blindfold, blinking rapidly to focus. The room I was in was gloomy, with blue painted walls and a dirty wooden floor. The room was empty apart from a chair and a table, with a newspaper and a squashed beer can on it. The window had had planks of wood nailed across it. My kidnappers watched me. The silence in the room was deafening.

"W-What d'you want my Dad to do?" I'd already guessed what they were after, but if I could speak then I was alive. And if I was alive, then I could get out of this. I *could*.

The two men smiled slyly at each other.

"Let's just say, we want him to make a delivery," said the blond man.

"And he'd better not mess us about either," said Baldy.

"A d-delivery ...?" I stammered.

"Yeah!" Baldy grinned. "One that ..."

"Shut up, Quill!" the blond man snapped harshly.

So now I knew the bald guy's real name.

"No names in front of the girl – remember?" the woman hissed.

They all turned to look at me. I couldn't help it, I burst into tears. The harder I tried to stop, the faster they fell. If Dad was here instead of you, he wouldn't cry, I told myself. Nothing could ever make Dad cry.

"Tie her up," said the woman, after a pause.

"I'll do it," said Quill.

I wondered if I could make a break for it. I could get past the two men, but the woman was

right by the door. Then the woman walked over to Quill and whispered in his ear. I took a deep breath. It was now or never.

Quill moved forward to stand in front of me and the chance to make a break for it slipped away. Would I get another?

Chapter 4
Held to Ransom

"When you've finished come downstairs," said the woman. "I want to talk to you – *both* of you."

The woman and the blond man left the room. I heard them walk downstairs. I turned around.

"Don't tie me up, Quill," I whispered. "I couldn't bear it."

"I've got no choice," he said gruffly. "And I'd forget that name if I were you. Don't use it in front of the others."

I shook my head. I wasn't that stupid.

"Are you... after the jewels in Dad's shop? Is that the d-delivery you were all talking about?" I asked.

Quill took some thin, plastic rope out of his jacket pocket before nodding. My heart sank to my toe nails at the sight of it. Dad used the same kind for wrapping parcels at home. It was thin but very strong, almost unbreakable.

"Once we get the jewels, we'll let you go. I promise," said Quill.

"And if Dad doesn't hand them over?"

"He wants you back, doesn't he?"

And the question turned my blood cold, because that was the problem. *I didn't know.* Dad loved his shop and his jewels. Dad always retreated to his shop when the quarrels between him and Mum became too bitter. Many times I'd watched him dust the displays of gold and silver necklaces, lovingly polish the gold rings, dust off the expensive gem stones. It had actually made me feel jealous. Then I felt foolish and incredibly angry for being jealous of bits of metal and fancy glass.

"Come on. This won't take long. Put your hands behind your back," Quill ordered.

With reluctance I did as I was told. Then I remembered something Dad had once told me, something else he'd learnt in the army. Keeping my wrists together, I bent my hands back, with my palms as far apart from each other as I could get them. Quill tied my wrists together, tight. I sat down, then he tied my ankles. I tried to keep my ankles together and my feet apart, flexing my feet upwards. Dad told me that if someone is tying you up, they'll need more rope to tie your hands and legs if you tense your muscles and flex your hands and feet. That way, when you relaxed, the ropes would be looser than if you relaxed to begin with. When Quill had finished he stood up.

"Do I have to gag you?" he asked.

I shook my head quickly. I couldn't bear the thought of something over my mouth.

"One single squeak out of you and I'll muzzle you like a dog."

I nodded.

"There's no use shouting or screaming, we're miles from anywhere. All you'll do is make the two downstairs very angry. D'you understand?" Quill said.

I nodded again. I heard footsteps, then the other two came back into the room. The woman was talking on a mobile phone.

"Mr Henshaw, you *will* do exactly as we say ... "

She stopped speaking.

I could hear Dad's furious voice at the other end of the line.

"Listen to me, Mr Henshaw," the woman interrupted. "I have someone here who'll force you to change your mind. Say hello to your father, Angela."

She thrust the phone against my ear.

"Dad ..." I whispered. "Dad, is that you?"

"Angela ...?" Dad was shocked. "Angela, are you all right?"

"Dad, I'm frightened ..." The phone was yanked away from me.

"That's enough," said the woman. She and the blond man left the room, the woman talking urgently into the phone.

"Like I said, behave yourself and you'll be home before you know it," said Quill.

He left the room, locking the door behind him.

I forced myself to relax. Immediately, the rope round my wrists felt looser. Then I lay down on the floor, desperate not to make a sound. I lay on my side and curled up tightly

into a ball, until I could slip my tied hands past my hips and down the backs of my legs. I slipped my feet heels first through the circle made by my arms. It didn't take long, I'm very supple. Sitting up again, I worked away at the rope binding my feet. The rope cut into my fingers as I worked to unknot it, but at last it fell away from my ankles. Untying my hands was trickier. I had to use my teeth and the index finger of one hand and the thumb of the other to prise the knot open. But I did it.

Now what?

I stood up and tip-toed over to the window. That was no good. There was no way I could pull away the boards that covered the window without making a real racket.

Think ... think ... think ... I looked in my pockets, hoping that something in there would give me an idea. I looked around. My mind was still a blank. I tip-toed across to the door. Even though I'd heard Quill lock the door, I turned the door knob anyway. Nothing. But then, what did I expect? I peeked through the key hole, trying to see if anyone was on the landing guarding my door, but I couldn't see a thing. On the other side of the door, the key was in the lock.

That's when an idea crept into my head. It was a very dangerous idea ...

I crept across the room to get the newspaper. I laid it flat, then pushed it under the door, so that it was half on my side of the door, with the other half on the landing. I shuffled the newspaper around so it was directly underneath the key. I put a stick of chewing gum in my mouth, to make it soft. I straightened out one of the safety pins I had and started poking about in the lock. The key began to shift backwards until it dropped out of the lock, landing with a clink on the newspaper. I held my breath. Had the kidnappers heard? Quickly I pulled the newspaper through to my

side of the door. The key was there on the newspaper. I froze, expecting to hear them rush up the stairs at any moment.

Silence.

I unlocked the door, opening it until it was almost touching the wall. I chewed harder on my chewing gum. Now came the hardest part of all. I ran to the window and started banging my fists on it.

"Help ... HELP!" I screamed at the top of my lungs.

At once I heard footsteps thundering up the stairs.

Please let it be all of them ... I prayed.

I raced across the room to stand behind the door. I wiped my sweaty hands on my coat, grasping the key to me.

"You were supposed to tie her up," the woman said furiously.

"I did," I heard Quill answer.

"The door's wide open," said the blond man.

They all raced in. This was it. I darted around the door and pulled it shut, jamming the key into the lock as I pulled it. My kidnappers shouted at me and the blond man lunged at the door as it closed, rage on his face. Frantically I turned the key in the lock.

Chapter 5
The Chase

Only just in time. The door knob rattled violently. Quickly taking the chewing gum out of my mouth, I stuffed it into the key hole. I used the end of the pencil to push it right in.

"Get out of the way. I've got a spare key," I heard the woman say.

For the first time since they'd captured me, I allowed myself a slight smile. I hadn't known for certain that they had a spare key. I'd just thought I'd better play safe. But now the woman's spare key wouldn't do her much good, not with the chewing gum and my pencil in the lock.

"Angela, open this door. NOW!" the blond man demanded.

Yeah! Likely! I thought. And raced down the stairs. I didn't have much time.

There it was – what I'd been looking for. *The telephone* ...

The others were still shouting at me from upstairs. The door knob rattled as they tried to open the door.

I picked up the receiver. Where would Dad be? At home or his shop? I didn't have time to find out. It would be faster to phone the police. I dialled 999 and asked the emergency operator for the police. Upstairs, they were now trying to batter the door down. At last I was put through.

"Please help me. My name's Angela Henshaw. My Dad owns Henshaw's Jewellers in the High Street. Listen! I've been kidnapped. The kidnappers left Deansea by the old church road.

We drove for about three minutes straight, then six hundred left, fourteen hundred right, one hundred and twenty right. No! Don't interrupt! Ask Dad, he'll tell you what it means!" I rushed on urgently as the voice at the other end tried to cut in. "I've been kidnapped and I don't know where ..."

But at that moment, the upstairs door splintered. The noise crashed through the house. The next second lasted forever. It was as if the very air in the house froze.

Then everything happened at once. I heard shouting. And then came footsteps running. I could just about hear it over the sound of my heart thundering. I didn't wait to hear any more. Almost blind with panic, I threw myself at the front door. My hands were all thumbs as I frantically pulled at the door latch.

Don't turn around ... I kept telling myself that over and over. It was as if, by not turning around, I could stop my kidnappers from catching me.

The door opened. It must have taken only a second, two at the most but that's not how it felt.

"ANGELA ...!"

"COME BACK HERE ..."

From somewhere close behind me came the voices of Baldy and the woman.

Don't turn around ...

Fingers touched my shoulder. I screamed and, head bent, charged towards the moonlit trees as fast as I could. I had to get away before whoever it was could get a good grip. Then the

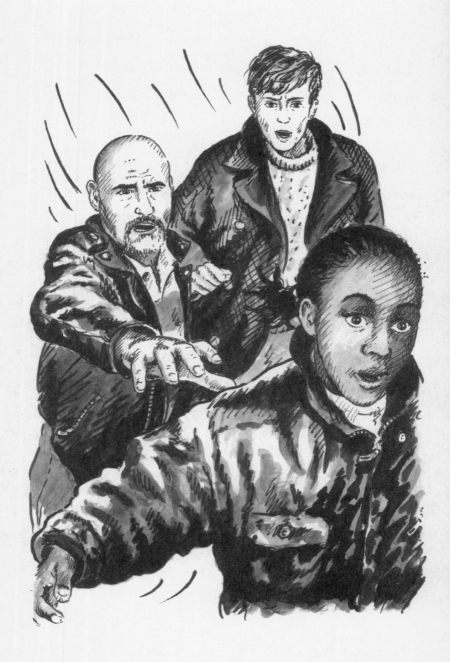

moon vanished behind a cloud and I couldn't see my hand in front of my face, but I didn't care. If I had to choose between the dark and the kidnappers, then the dark would win hands down.

"ANGELA, WE WON'T HURT YOU ..."

"DAMN IT! COME BACK ..."

Their voices seemed to come from everywhere at once. For all I knew I might be about to head-butt one of them in the stomach. Good!

Don't look back, Angela. Keep running.

I slipped, then clambered up immediately and kept on running. I ran and ran until I thought my lungs would burst like balloons –

and still I kept running. I couldn't hear their voices any more. It didn't matter.

And then the ground disappeared. I started falling and falling. It was like falling through space or falling in slow motion. I thought I'd never stop.

Chapter 6
Cliffhanger

I must have been knocked out. I woke up as
if from a really bad nightmare, the worst
nightmare I'd ever had in my life. Except that it
was still dark and bitterly cold – and very real.
My whole body ached. I couldn't see a thing. But
I could sense that something wasn't quite right.
I shifted around slightly, feeling about with my
hands. There was about forty centimetres of
solid ledge in front of me and after that ...
nothing. I was on this long, thin ledge

somewhere and goodness only knew how long the drop was beyond that.

What was left of my courage vanished.

"HELP!" I screamed at the top of my voice. I stretched up and shouted again. "HELP!"

The ledge moved. I actually felt the ledge shake and shift slightly.

I couldn't breathe. I was choking on terror. Slowly, I felt behind me for a hand hold. There was none. And I was so cold and getting worse. I felt so tired. All I wanted to do was sleep. But I remembered Dad telling me once that if you were stuck outside somewhere and really cold, one of the worst things you could do was give in to it and go to sleep. "Do that and you might never wake up again," he said.

Dad ... If only I could see him one more time just to hug him and say ... sorry.

"DAD ..." I shouted desperately.

"ANGELA? ANGELA!"

And then there was a light shining in my eyes, dazzling me.

"Angela, hang on. I'm here with the police. You've fallen part of the way down Deansea quarry. Stay still. We're coming down to get you."

I couldn't help it. I started crying again, sobbing even harder than before. It was Dad.

Dad had come to get me.

In the torch light above, I saw a policeman tie a rope around his waist.

"Angela, I'm Police Sergeant Kent. It's all right. I'm coming to get you, so don't run off will you!"

That made me laugh a bit, even though I was still crying. Dad and the other policemen and women then held on to the other end of the rope. Sergeant Kent came down for me and lifted me like a sack of potatoes onto his shoulder. Then he climbed back up the quarry face. Dad lifted me off the policeman's back before my feet even touched the ground. I don't know which was tighter – Dad hugging me, or me hugging Dad. My cheek against Dad's was wet, but I wasn't the one crying. There were three policemen and a policewoman around us, shining torches at us and grinning like a row of smiley faces.

"Dad, d-did you give the kidnappers your jewels?" I asked in a whisper.

"Angela, I would have given them everything I had to get you back home safely," Dad smiled.

"How did you know where to find me?" I sniffed.

"We got to your father just as he was about to leave his shop with two carrier bags filled with jewels for the kidnappers. He was able to understand your coded message," said the policeman closest to us.

Dad and I smiled at each other.

"Really, sir, you should have got in touch with us right away," said Sergeant Kent to Dad. "We in the police know how to handle things like this."

"I didn't want to risk it," Dad said. "Angela means more to me than all the jewels in the world."

"Where are the kidnappers?" I asked.

"We've got them all!" grinned the policewoman. "They still don't understand how you could have told us about their hideaway as you were blindfolded throughout the drive up here!"

"Why don't you two leave now. Our questions can wait until tomorrow," said Sergeant Kent.

"Dad, can we go home?" I whispered.

"I'll cook you your favourite dinner of beans, bangers and mash while you have a bath and get warm. Then we'll talk. OK?"

"OK," I grinned. That was all I'd ever wanted.

And we walked hand in hand back to Dad's car.

BLACKMAN, MALORIE
HOSTAGE

C12106
JUN
FIC
BLA

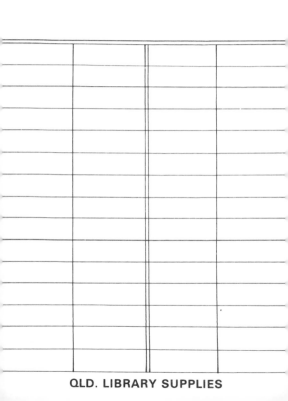

QLD. LIBRARY SUPPLIES

DUE BACK

Other Barrington Stoke titles available

What's Going On, Gus? by Jill Atkins 1-902260-10

Ghost for Sale by Terry Deary 1-902260-14-7

Billy the Squid by Colin Dowland 1-902260-04-X

Kick Back by Vivian French 1-902260-02-3

The Gingerbread House by Adèle Geras 1-902260-0

Virtual Friend by Mary Hoffman 1-902260-00-7

Tod in Biker City by Anthony Masters 1-902260-15-5

Wartman by Michael Morpurgo 1-902260-05-8

Extra Time by Jenny Oldfield 1-902260-13-9

Screw Loose by Alison Prince 1-902260-01-5

Lift Off by Hazel Townson 1-902260-11-2

If you would like more information about the **BARRINGTON STOKE CLUB**, please write to:- Barrington Stoke Club, 10 Belford Terrace, Edinburgh, EH4 3DQ or visit our website at:-
www.barringtonstoke.co.uk